Quiz # 163455
BL: 4.9
PTS: 3

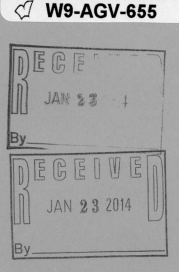

W9-AGV-655

RECEIVED
JAN 23 4
By_____

RECEIVED
JAN 23 2014
By_____

Just Grace and the Super Sleepover

Just Grace and the Super Sleepover

Written and illustrated
by
Charise Mericle Harper

HOUGHTON MIFFLIN HARCOURT
Boston   New York

www.hmhbooks.com

The text of this book is set in Dante MT.
The illustrations are pen-and-ink drawings digitally colored in Photoshop.

Library of Congress Cataloging-in-Publication Data
Harper, Charise Mericle, author, illustrator.
Just Grace and the super sleepover / written and illustrated by
Charise Mericle Harper.
p. cm.
Summary: Just Grace is excited to attend her classmate Grace F.'s sleepover
birthday party until she learns it will be a camp-out, and then her fears begin
to cause trouble.
ISBN 978-0-544-04584-2
[1. Schools—Fiction. 2. Friendship—Fiction. 3. Fear—Fiction. 4. Honesty—Fiction. 5. Camping—Fiction. 6. Sleepovers—Fiction. 7. Birthdays—Fiction.]
I. Title.
PZ7.H231323Jue 2014
[Fic]—dc23
2013004813

Manufactured in the United States of America
DOC 10 9 8 7 6 5 4 3 2 1

4500449119

For my friend Laurie Keller, who likes Grace
and is a super sleepover guest.

THINGS THAT ARE UNUSUAL ABOUT ME

1. At school my teacher calls me Just Grace instead of Grace. This kind of thing can happen if your teacher is not paying attention when you say, *Please call me just Grace.*

2. My best friend lives right next door to me, and I can see her bedroom window from my bedroom window.

3. I have a flight attendant living in the apartment in my basement. Her name is Augustine Dupre, and she lives there with her husband, Luke. Augustine Dupre is super nice and her apartment is amazing and beautiful.

4. I have a dog that is a girl dog, but she has a boy-dog name. Her name is Mr. Scruffers. When I adopted her I tried to change her

name, but it was too hard. She loves being called Mr. Scruffers.

5. I have a teeny-tiny superpower. It's empathy power, and every time someone is sad or unhappy it starts working, and I have to help them feel better. Empathy power is not an easy superpower to live with— sometimes it can get you into trouble, but if I'm lucky it works out just fine.

HOW MY EMPATHY POWER WORKS

WHAT IS STRANGE

Sometimes even if you know that something is true, you can still have trouble believing it. That's how I felt when Miss Lois was showing us the globe of the world, and talking about the earth spinning. I should have been listening, but it's hard to do two things at once, especially if one of those things is trying to figure out if you might be hanging upside down.

Miss Lois is good at noticing stuff, because even though I was being careful and only moving when she was looking away, she still saw me. This was unlucky, because Miss Lois is not the kind of teacher who just nods and gives you a silent I-need-you-to-pay-attention look. She's loud. If you get caught doing something wrong in her class, everyone is going to know about it. That's why as soon as she stopped talking and looked at me, I knew I was in trouble. Miss Lois pointed her finger and said, "Just Grace, stop fidgeting in your seat and pay attention." As soon as she said that, everyone in the whole class

NOT FUN

HAVING EVERYONE STARE AT YOU WHEN YOU GET IN TROUBLE

turned around and looked at me. This kind of attention is not the same as getting attention when you are on stage.

FUN

BEING ON STAGE

I put my head down and stared at the eraser on my desk until my face felt normal, and not hot and red anymore. When I looked up, everyone was back to looking at Miss Lois, except for one person, but that was okay, because I was expecting it. I looked across the room and found Mimi. She nodded her head and gave me a big you'll-be-okay smile. Instantly I started to feel better. It was the exact right thing for a best friend to do.

Owen 1 says that the reason that Miss Lois is good at noticing stuff is because she has fly eyes. Of course that's 100 percent crazy and not true, but when Owen 1 says weird stuff, it's better to pretend you didn't hear him. Arguing with Owen 1 is not a good idea. He's a bad loser.

WHAT FLY EYES WOULD LOOK LIKE

Sometimes when I am mad or upset I like to draw comics. I don't know why it works, but it usually helps me feel better. I did that the last time Owen 1 was a bad loser, and when I was done I felt almost 100 percent better, plus it was fun to draw him saying he was sorry. Even if something doesn't happen in real life, it can help you feel better just imagining it.

WHAT HAPPENED

Of course the fantasy ending didn't really happen—instead what really happened was that Owen 1 just looked at me with a mean face and then walked away. I knew he wasn't one bit sorry.

I was thinking about that comic when suddenly someone poked me in the back with a pencil. That kind of thing is impossible to ignore, especially when you know who the someone is and they are not one of your favorite people. Owen 1 sits right behind me, and every time he doesn't understand something, wants to tell me a stupid joke, or is bored, he pokes me. I've told Miss Lois about it a million times, but it doesn't make a difference.

CIRCLE OF NOTHING HAPPENING

After a while, instead of Owen 1 stopping poking me, it was me who did the stopping. I stopped complaining.

RULE OF COMPLAINING

If you complain about someone a lot, the person who you are complaining to will start to get annoyed by all your complaining, and suddenly you might be the one who is getting into trouble instead of the person who is doing the thing that you are complaining about. Sometimes when something sounds complicated a drawing can make it easier to understand.

DRAWING THAT EXPLAINS
THE RULE OF COMPLAINING

These kinds of rules are not fair, but sometimes in life, unfair things happen.

MY NEW PLAN FOR HANDLING OWEN 1

When Owen 1 pokes me, I spin around and try to grab his pencil away from him before he can pull it back. At first this was really hard to do, but he pokes me a lot so I've had lots of practice, and I've gotten better. If I can get his pencil, I break the lead off and then drop the pencil back on his desk. This works perfectly, because Miss Lois doesn't like people walking up to the front of the class and using the pencil sharpener when she is in the middle of talking. So if she gets mad at Owen 1 and he gets into trouble, it's kind of fair.

THE REASON OWEN 1 WAS POKING ME

To ask me if I thought we were hanging upside down right this minute and didn't even know it. This was a surprise. I wasn't expecting him to be thinking the same thing as me. And if we were both thinking it, then probably lots of other people were thinking it too. I looked around the class, but you can't tell what people are thinking just by looking at them. I wish you could. It would be cool if people had bubbles above their heads, like they do in comics. But I'd only want them to last for a second, because longer than a second is probably too much information.

READING MINDS FOR A SECOND — GOOD

Sometimes, right things can suddenly turn into wrong things. That's what happened with Owen 1's pencil. Now I felt bad that I'd broken his pencil. I thought he was just poking me to be annoying, but now that I knew that he had the same thoughts as me, it made things different. So for this time only, when I gave him back his pencil I gave him one of my extra pencils too. That way he wouldn't have to go up front and sharpen his broken one and get into trouble with Miss Lois. It was good that Miss Lois was busy looking for something in her desk or we would have for sure gotten into trouble.

PENCILS CHOICES FOR OWEN 1

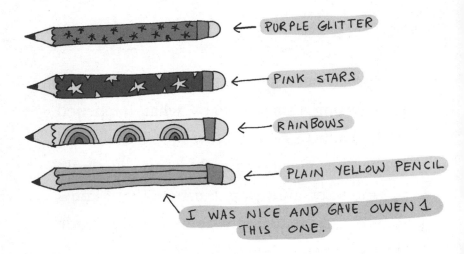

← PURPLE GLITTER

← PINK STARS

← RAINBOWS

← PLAIN YELLOW PENCIL

I WAS NICE AND GAVE OWEN 1 THIS ONE.

MISS LOIS AND THE EARTH

Miss Lois doesn't just love the earth because it is round. She said round is a nice shape, but the reason she really loves the earth is because it has so many amazing features.

Of course no one knew what she was talking about, so she had to explain that she was meaning all the shapes that make the earth look the way it does. Things like mountains, valleys, oceans, and continents, and we were going to learn about all of them. When you study the physical features of the earth, that is called geography, and that's what Miss Lois was really in love with.

She said we were all going to love geography as much as she did, and then she smiled really big so we could all see how excited she was. After she said that, I could tell what was coming next. Miss Lois was making a team-up of love and learning. That kind of team-up can take all the fun out of love, but I made myself stay quiet and not say anything.

It's not a good idea to tell a teacher that their idea is a bad one. Teachers are a little like Owen 1—they don't like to hear about their mistakes. But at least they don't throw things.

When Miss Lois was sure that everyone looked excited about learning about the earth, she told us all about what we were going to do. She said we were going to make special books filled with earth facts. Then she went to her desk and pulled out one of the books. It looked like a regular notebook, except instead of being rectangular-shaped, it was rounded like the earth. Miss Lois said a friend of hers had made them by cutting off all the corners of the notebooks with his saw. I don't know why, but round notebooks suddenly made Miss Lois's project a lot more exciting.

REGULAR NOTEBOOK

NOTEBOOK MORE ROUND LIKE THE EARTH

WHAT HAPPENED AT LUNCH

Mimi and I ate lunch together like usual. It's nice when something is a pattern and you don't have to worry about it. The only thing I have to worry about at lunchtime is what kind of sandwich I have. Mom hates making lunches, and if I didn't complain, she'd give me the exact same sandwich every day for the whole year.

MIMI EATING HER LUNCH.

I LIKE CHEESE SANDWICHES, BUT I DON'T WANT TO EAT THEM EVERY DAY.

ANOTHER CHEESE SANDWICH.

Sunni's mom is the exact opposite of Mom. She loves making lunches. In fact, she loves it so much, she took a special course to learn how to do it better. Sunni says that the course was definitely worth it, because before her mom went to bento box school, she used to only get leftovers, but now she gets masterpieces instead.

NORMAL LUNCH

BORING SANDWICH

CARROT STICKS

YOGURT

BENTO LUNCH

CARROT HAIR

SPACE SHIP MADE OUT OF FRUIT

ALIEN SANDWICH

RED PEPPER ARMS AND LEGS

RICE

LETTUCE

Pretty much everyone is jealous of Sunni's new lunches—even the boys. Sunni's mom has only been making them for about a week, but they're already kind of famous. Sunni says the only part she doesn't like is that everyone wants to see them. She says it's hard to be excited about eating a lunch after everyone has breathed on it.

Today Sunni's lunch was an alien—it was one of my favorites. So far she's eaten a smiling sun, an underwater scene, a panda, a character from her favorite video game, and her own name in big fancy letters. I don't know how all those things tasted, but they looked amazing.

Sunni said bento boxes are a big thing in Japan, and Japanese mothers like to make them as a way of showing their children how much they love them. As soon as she said that, Mimi said, "Well, your mom must really love you." Sunni nodded, smiled, and then picked up her alien sandwich. "She does," said Sunni. "But she also loves craft projects,

so it kind of works out well for both of us."
I thought she might say something else, but
she didn't—she just bit off the alien's head.
A lot of boys were smiling and watching her.
None of them said anything, but I knew ex-
actly what they were thinking.

When I first saw Sunni's bento lunches, I
told Mom all about them and how much Sunni's mom loved making them for her. I was
hoping it would make her excited and get the
idea to make one for me, but she just shook

her head and said she was glad she wasn't Japanese. It wasn't a complete no, but it wasn't a yes either. I had a feeling bento lunches were not in my future.

THE SONG WE LEARNED AFTER LUNCH

If Miss Lois ever gets tired of being a teacher, she could get a new job as a professional singer. I didn't know this before, but she has a great singing voice. Even though she only sang us a baby song, I could still tell that she was good. Miss Lois said she made up the baby song to help our brains remember the names of the seven continents on the earth.

Remembering seven new things is not easy, especially if you haven't thought about them before. Some kids were kind of embarrassed about standing up and doing hand motions, but that was crazy, because moving around was a lot more fun than sitting at our desks. Plus Miss Lois said that when we had the earth test we were allowed to move our arms and hands around to help us remember everything. Robert Walters asked if we were going to be allowed to stand up and sing during the test, but I already knew the answer to that. Most of Robert Walters's questions end up with the same answer from Miss Lois. It's not a spoken out loud answer but it means no—she shakes her head and scrunches her eyebrows down.

MISS LOIS'S NORMAL FACE

MISS LOIS'S FACE AFTER LISTENING TO ROBERT WALTERS

Miss Lois changed the words from a real song that we already knew and made it about the continents instead. Sometimes she can be kind of smart.

The Real Song

Head, shoulders,
Knees and toes,

Knees and toes
Head, shoulders,
Knees and toes,
Knees and toes.
Eyes and ears and mouth and nose,
Head, shoulders, knees and toes, knees and
toes!

Our Song

Europe, Asia,
North and South
America
Europe, Asia,
North and South
America
Africa, Antarctica, Australia
Europe, Asia,
North and South
America

(HEAD) EUROPE

AFRICA (EYES)

ANTARCTICA (EARS)

AUSTRALIA (MOUTH + NOSE)

(SHOULDERS) ASIA

(KNEES)

NORTH AMERICA ← WE DON'T SAY THIS AMERICA IN THE SONG.

SOUTH AMERICA

(TOES)

Once we were done with the continents, I thought we'd be done with the earth, but Miss Lois said that we had to learn the oceans of the world too. There are only five of them, but it was harder than the continents, because she didn't have a song. I wanted to ask why, but Owen 1 surprised me and asked the question before I could even put my hand up. This was the second time that Owen 1 and I were thinking the exact same things. What was going on? Was he reading my mind? I hoped not. This was not a super skill I was excited about him having.

MISS LOIS'S SURPRISES

After we wrote down the oceans of the world Miss Lois surprised us with an announcement. "Next week we're going to have a surprise guest in our classroom." Of course everyone wanted to know who it was, but she wouldn't even give us any clues. Robert Walters put his hand up and asked, "Is it going to be the president?" Miss Lois looked surprised for a second, and then she shook her head. That was too bad—the president would be a surprise guest I'd be excited to meet.

Today should have been called surprise day, because as soon as Miss Lois finished telling us about the guest surprise, she surprised us again.

CLASS, WE ARE GOING TO BE WORKING ON OUR NOTEBOOKS, BUT THAT'S NOT ALL. WE ARE ALSO DOING A PROJECT WITH A PARTNER.

Usually when Miss Lois says this kind of thing, I get nervous. Miss Lois is not a you-can-pick-your-own-partner kind of person. Having a partner can be super fun if you're excited about the person you are working with. But not all partners are the same. Sometimes certain people make you feel uncomfortable. I was hoping that Owen 1 was not reading my mind again, because my brain was making a list and his name was on it.

PEOPLE I DON'T WANT AS A PARTNER

So I guess it's good that thoughts can't be heard, because a lot of people would get their feelings hurt. Thinking about Owen 1 and his mind-reading skills made me suddenly feel sad for real mind readers. Mind reading is probably a really hard superpower to live with.

WHAT MIMI AND I PRACTICED ON THE WAY HOME FROM SCHOOL

The continents. It was fun to sing the song.

WHAT WE WOULD NOT HAVE PRACTICED IF IT WAS JUST A LIST TO MEMORIZE

The continents. Sometimes Miss Lois is a teaching genius.

WHAT HAPPENED WHEN I GOT HOME

1. I said goodbye to Mimi (that took two seconds).
2. I said hello to Mr. Scruffers (that took twenty minutes).

If you are your dog's favorite person in the whole world, you have to be good about spending time with her, even if you are sometimes tired and maybe don't always feel like it. When I leave for school in the morning, Mr. Scruffers has to wait for more than twenty-six thousand seconds until she gets to see me again. That's a long time, and that kind of waiting deserves a lot of attention.

Mr. Scruffers's favorite thing to do is to chase squirrels. I got her a ball that looks like a squirrel, but I think she can tell that difference.

IT'S NOT A REAL SQUIRREL BUT I LIKE IT.

BALL THAT LOOKS LIKE SQUIRREL

Mr. Scruffers is good about bringing the ball back. She's not one of those dogs who keep the ball in their mouth and then run off with it every time you get close to taking it away. Those kinds of dogs are annoying—to get the ball you have to stick your hand in their mouth and yank it out. Even though I love Mr. Scruffers, I think I would have a hard time with that. A person can only take so much dog slobber.

AMOUNT OF SLOBBER NORMALLY ON MR. SCRUFFERS'S BALL.

AMOUNT OF SLOBBER ON A BALL FROM A DOG WHO KEEPS THE BALL IN THEIR MOUTH

If I had mind-reading skills, Mr. Scruffers's brain would be one of the first brains I'd want to read.

After I finished playing with Mr. Scruffers I went inside, and right away I saw a letter for me, waiting on the kitchen table.

THE LETTER

Before I even opened it, I knew exactly who it was from and what it was for. It was an invitation to Grace F.'s birthday sleepover. Grace F. is not very good at surprises. She's not like Miss Lois. As soon as her mom said she could have a birthday sleepover, she told everyone who was going to be invited all about it. I opened the envelope, pulled out the card, and then suddenly I was the one who was surprised.

Some people like to sleep outside and do camping things, but I am not one of those people. In my whole life, I have never slept outside before—and suddenly just thinking about it was making me nervous.

THINGS THAT ARE DIFFERENT BETWEEN SLEEPING INSIDE AND SLEEPING OUTSIDE

SLEEPING INSIDE

1- NOTHING WILL BITE YOU.
2- NOTHING WILL EAT YOU.
3- STRANGE ANIMALS ARE NOT WALKING AROUND IN YOUR HOUSE.

SLEEPING OUTSIDE

1. BUGS WILL BITE YOU.
2. A BEAR COULD EAT YOU.
3. ANIMALS ARE WALKING AROUND IN THE DARK.

When you are nervous and uncomfortable, sometimes a mom can help. I looked around the house until I found Mom. I had lots of questions.

Is it legal to sleep in a backyard?
Do bears live around here?
What kind of bugs come out at night?

If you are going to be attacked by a wolf, does it howl first to warn you?
Is Grace F.'s house near a graveyard?

Mom said she was pretty sure I didn't have to worry about creatures or ghosts. I nodded, but still I would have been happier if the invitation was for more than just me. A dog is a good thing to have with you if you are worried about sleeping outside.

WHAT I DIDN'T GET TO SAY
TO MR. SCRUFFERS

YOU'RE INVITED TOO! YOU CAN PROTECT ME.

WILL THERE BE LOTS OF SNACKS?

I felt a little better when Mom said she'd call Grace F.'s mom to ask about the party.

THE PARTY FACTS MOM FOUND OUT

1. We are all going to sleep in one big tent.
2. Grace F.'s big sister Stephanie is going to sleep outside with us.
3. We are going to have a campfire and make

s'mores, but Grace F.'s dad is going to be there, so Mom said she wasn't worried about the fire.

I didn't say anything, but Mom's facts didn't make me feel any better. Instead of them being gone, my worries were even bigger, and suddenly I had a new question.

Is Grace F.'s big sister nice?

THE SURPRISE AT THE DOOR

Mimi knocking on my door is never a surprise. We are best friends, and she is always coming over, but today there was a surprise part, and it had to do with the sleepover. Mimi wasn't like me, because as soon as I opened the door, she waved her party invitation in the air and said, "This is going to be the best party ever! Aren't you super excited?" Mimi's little brother, Robert, was standing next to her, and I let them both in. I smiled and nodded to answer her question. The time didn't seem exactly right to tell her the truth about how I was feeling. Robert walked in ahead of Mimi. He looked grumpy. "I want to sleep outside," he said. Mimi shook her head. "Ignore him," she said. "He's jealous."

Robert nodded. Now he looked even sadder, but then he tugged at my sleeve and looked up at me. "Beetles come out at night. Will you catch some for me?" he asked. Instantly Mimi was scowling. She put her hands on her hips and glared down at him. "Robert, I already told you, we're not going bug hunting. It's a party, and Grace is like me—she won't have time to look for beetles." Robert ignored her. He poked me to make sure I was paying attention to him and then spread his hands apart. "The titan beetle can grow this big," he said. I scrunched up my face and looked at Mimi. She nodded. "It's true," she said. "It can be seven inches long, but don't worry, it doesn't live here." "It's a rainforest bug," complained Robert. "All the good stuff lives in the rainforest." I didn't say anything, but I was glad about that, and doubly glad that the rainforest was far away from my house.

Talking about bugs was not a good idea. It was not helping me be excited about the sleepover—in fact, it was doing the exact opposite. I had to get rid of Robert so we could change the subject. I pointed to the back door. "Robert, why don't you go outside and play with Mr. Scruffers." Robert smiled and ran to the door, but before he went outside, he turned around and gave me one more beetle fact. "Did you know there are thousands of different kinds of beetles that live right here where we do?" It was exactly the kind of fact I didn't want to know about.

MIMI

Usually when Mimi comes over we talk about a million different things, but today all she wanted to talk about was the sleepover. I tried to change the subject, but every time I did, she just changed it back again. And then after a while of agreeing with her about how exciting it was, it was too late to tell her the truth.

Mimi knew a lot more about the party than I did, so at least that was interesting. Five girls were invited: me, Mimi, Grace L., Marta, and a girl we didn't know named Lisa. Mimi said Lisa was a girl in Grace F.'s Wednesday afterschool art class. I was wondering how come Mimi knew so much about the party, but before I could ask her, she gave me the answer. She said she'd opened her invitation the minute she got home from school and then called Grace F. right away to tell her she was coming. Having Mom call had been a huge mistake—she didn't get any of the good or important details.

WE ARE GOING TO DECORATE A STUFFED ANIMAL, WATCH A MOVIE OUTSIDE, EAT S'MORES, AND MAYBE EVEN BOUNCE ON GRACE F.'S TRAMPOLINE.

BUT MY FAVORITE PART IS THE SLEEPING OUTSIDE.

Mimi's favorite thing about the party was the number one thing I didn't like. It was weird to have us feeling so different about it. I wanted to make myself be like her, and be excited, but I couldn't. Just thinking about being in the dark, with creatures all around, made my ears hot and my hands sweaty. Plus now I was worried about beetles, too!

I was a good actress though, because Mimi didn't even notice. I think that can happen when you are really excited about something—your paying-attention skills don't work as well. Mimi had all sorts of ideas about the party. Suddenly she looked at me and said, "Let's get up in the middle of the night and go outside and look up at the stars. Wouldn't that be amazing?" I nodded, but my insides were not agreeing with my outsides. My insides were thinking all sorts of things that I was not saying out loud.

WHAT IS A LIE

Even though school is for learning, it doesn't teach you everything. Right now I could name the earth's seven continents, but that wasn't one bit helpful when I was trying to figure out if nodding my head counts as a lie or not. And if it does count, is it as bad as a speaking lie? And if you only say a one-word lie, is that as bad as a whole-sentence lie?

WHAT WAS NOT NORMAL

Usually when Mimi comes over I am sad to see her leave, but today was different. Today I couldn't wait for her mom to call and tell her she had to come home for dinner. My head was spinning, and I wanted to stop talking about, and even thinking about, the sleepover. I was 100 percent wishing that Grace F. had picked something different for her birthday, something regular and normal, like skating or bowling.

NIGHTTIME

Mimi's bedroom window is right across from mine, so at night before we go to bed we flash our lights at each other. Usually we do it three times, and as I flash the light on and off, I always say the same three words, "See you tomorrow." But tonight I said something different: I said words I had never said before.

WHAT IS HARD TO DO

Go to sleep when all you can think about is giant beetles. It helped that Mr. Scruffers was sleeping next to me, but still, it took a lot longer to fall asleep than normal. Finally, since I couldn't stop thinking about them, I had to imagine that the giant beetles were wearing tutus and doing a dance routine. It definitely made them less scary. Too bad that kind of thing couldn't happen in real life.

← VERY GOOD DANCERS

WALKING TO SCHOOL

Mimi and I always walk to school together. Even before she came over, I knew what she would want to be talking about—the sleepover. She was excited about it, and when you are excited about something, you can't help but talk about it. I was not like her. When you are not excited about something, all you want to do is ignore it and pretend it doesn't exist. This was not going to be an easy walk.

I was waiting and ready to go when Mimi knocked on my door. I yelled goodbye to Mom and followed Mimi outside. When we got to the sidewalk, she turned around and held out her hand. "Oh, I almost forgot," she said. "This is for you." I stepped closer to see what she was holding, and then screamed and ran back to the house. It was a giant bug. Mimi laughed and held it up by its leg. "It's not real, see? It's plastic. Robert wanted you to have it so you'd remember to get beetles."

She walked over to where I was standing and held her hand out so I could see it closer. I shook my head and took a step back. I didn't want to touch it. Mimi put it in her backpack and then gave me a strange look. "When did you get scared of bugs?" she asked. I shrugged and sighed. "It's a new thing," I said. It was true—being scared of bugs had just started, and it was all because of camping.

I was right about Mimi wanting to talk about the sleepover, but instead of talking about the tent, she wanted to tell me about the craft project we were going to do. Mimi loves crafts, so she was super excited that we were going to be making our own stuffed characters. At first I was worried that it was going to be all about sewing, but Mimi said it was more about gluing, so that was good. Of course Mimi would sew hers, even if she didn't have to—her hands loved sewing. My hands were happier about the glue.

OUR MORNING AT SCHOOL

Miss Lois was still filled with joy about the earth, and even though I was nervous about the sleepover and thinking my own thoughts, her joy snuck into me and made me feel better. We practiced the continents song a few more times, and then we learned where everything fit on the map. It wasn't as hard as I thought it was going to be, and I even got the oceans right.

When Miss Lois thought that everyone understood where everything went, she gave us our new earth notebooks. The first thing we did was glue in a map of the earth and then color and label all the continents and oceans. She said we could be creative, so I used fancy letters to write out the ocean names.

Of course Miss Lois was wrong about everyone knowing where everything went. Peter Marchelli sits in the desk across from me, and when I looked over at his map, I could tell that it was wrong. He put the Arctic Ocean under North America, and I don't think he was the only one, because after walking around the class to check our work, Miss Lois made us all stand up and put our arms out so we could learn about north, south, east, and west. The north and south part is easy to remember, but the east and the west parts were confusing. Miss Lois said that sometimes it's easier to remember something if you can think of a memory trick to go with it.

Some of the kids got confused about that, but I knew exactly what she meant, and I came up with some good ones to help me remember.

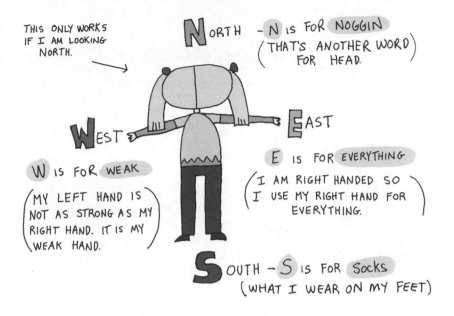

THIS ONLY WORKS IF I AM LOOKING NORTH.

NORTH — N IS FOR NOGGIN (THAT'S ANOTHER WORD FOR HEAD.

EAST

E IS FOR EVERYTHING (I AM RIGHT HANDED SO I USE MY RIGHT HAND FOR EVERYTHING.

WEST

W IS FOR WEAK (MY LEFT HAND IS NOT AS STRONG AS MY RIGHT HAND. IT IS MY WEAK HAND.)

SOUTH — S IS FOR SOCKS (WHAT I WEAR ON MY FEET)

SUNNI'S LUNCH

Today Sunni ate a flower and a bee. Some of the boys were disappointed that it wasn't something more crazy and weird, but still it was amazing. And even though we were all wishing we could have a lunch like Sunni's, it didn't feel like a bad jealousy.

GOOD JEALOUSY

After we were done eating, Grace F., Grace L., Marta, and me and Mimi all got together to talk about the birthday sleepover. Grace F. said we had to remember to bring sleeping bags and pillows, and then she told us all about the giant tent we were going to sleep in. She said the only bad part was that her sister Stephanie had to sleep in there with us too. "She snores," said Grace F., and then she did an impression of her sister snoring that made us all laugh. Grace L. didn't laugh very hard, but I couldn't tell what she was thinking about. And then right when the bell rang to go back inside, Grace L. said, "I'm not going to stay for the sleepover part. I don't like tents." For a second no one said anything, but then Grace F. asked, "Can you stay for everything else?" Grace L. nodded, and that was it. No one said one more word about it—they just went back to talking about the sleepover. I couldn't believe that no one was asking her tons of questions about what she had said, or trying to get her to change her mind. It was like the second she finished talking, everyone had forgotten what she had said. I wasn't like them. I was still thinking about it.

I DIDN'T KNOW WE COULD LEAVE EARLY.

COULD I DO THAT TOO? NOT STAY FOR THE SLEEPOVER?

NO, I COULDN'T LEAVE MIMI. SHE WOULD WANT ME TO BE THERE.

WHAT WAS GREAT ABOUT THE AFTERNOON

It went by super fast. That was good, because it's always nice to go home, but it was bad, too, because the faster the week went by, the sooner it would be Saturday—the day of the sleepover party.

Time really only goes by at one speed, but not everyone is always happy about that. Right now, sitting in this classroom, there was one person who wanted it to go super slow, and four people who wanted it to go fast.

The last thing that happened in the after-noon was that we all got earth project part-ners. When Miss Lois said, "It's time to pick partners," everyone groaned. The groaning was for one reason only—Miss Lois never lets us pick our own partners. But this time Miss Lois surprised us and said, "You can pick your own partners." Instantly the room was filled with everyone being excited, and talking and moving around. Of course my partner was going to be Mimi. She can move fast when she wants to. She was at my desk before I could even stand up.

WHAT WE GET TO DO WITH OUR PARTNERS THIS WEEK

1. Find out three facts about the continent or ocean we are assigned.
2. Use a compass to find a treasure.

As soon as Miss Lois said "treasure," everyone got excited.

But that didn't last very long, because
Miss Lois's treasure was not a real treasure. It
wasn't gold, or jewels, or money, or even anything a little bit good. It was only the word
treasure written on a piece of paper. It was
hard to stay excited about that.

WHAT MIMI'S BRAIN WAS THINKING ABOUT WHEN WE WERE WALKING HOME

As soon as Mimi told me her idea, I put my hand up and high-fived her. It was a great idea, and for sure it was going to make Grace F. feel special and happy, which was good, because having your birthday on a school day is not very exciting. On school birthdays only two fun things ever happen.

1. You get to bring in a special treat for the class to eat at snack time.

2. You get wished a happy birthday over the loudspeaker during the morning announcements.

Other than that, it's pretty much a regular, not very exciting school day.

WHAT HAPPENED WHEN I GOT HOME

I played with Mr. Scruffers. That's the good thing about having a dog: even if your brain is busy thinking of other things, you can still make your dog happy.

When dinner was over, I told Mom about the tent, and how I wasn't sure I was going to like it. It was too hard to keep it a secret anymore. I could tell that she was surprised, but what I was hoping for didn't come true—

she didn't have any ideas to help me. Mom is not a camper type person. She said she'd only ever slept in a tent once, when she was five years old. I shook my head. Mom being five years old was a long time ago, and when something's that far back, it's almost like it doesn't count.

That night Dad came to talk to me at bedtime. He's not a big camper either, but he was not like Mom—he had an idea.

DAD'S IDEA

1. Borrow a tent from a friend.
2. Sleep in the tent in the backyard on Friday night so I can get used to camping before the party happens.

The second after Dad told me his idea, I jumped up and gave him a huge hug. It was the kind of plan that was going to work, I could tell—plus how could I be scared about being outside when both Dad and Mr. Scruffers were going to be right there next to me? Dad's idea reminded me of something Augustine Dupre always says: *Practice makes perfect.* Suddenly I was feeling a whole lot better about things.

MAY BE CAMPING WON'T BE THAT BAD.

Before I went to bed I made two lists, one of all the things Dad and I could do, and one of all the things I didn't want to do. It was strange, but suddenly I was more excited about Friday than I was about Saturday.

THINGS TO DO IN THE TENT
1. SNACK.
2. HAVE DAD TELL ME A NICE, NOT SCARY STORY.
3. PLAY GAMES.

THINGS TO NOT DO IN THE TENT
1- TELL GHOST STORIES.
2- GO OUTSIDE THE TENT AND WALK AROUND.
3- MAKE ANIMAL NOISES.

That night at bedtime, when I flashed my lights at Mimi, I was back to using the normal words like I usually did. Of course Mimi couldn't tell the difference, because all she saw was three flashes, but to me the difference was huge.

WHAT WAS A SURPRISE IN THE MORNING

This morning I was just opening the door to walk outside when Mimi knocked. The first thing she asked me was, "Did you make your card for Grace F.?" The answer was no, I had totally forgotten about it, but that's not what I said. The word that came out of my mouth was a surprise. Without even thinking about it, my mouth said, "Yes." And once the yes was out, I couldn't take it back. I put my head down so Mimi couldn't see my face. She didn't notice. Instead she just talked about how surprised Grace F. was going to be with all her cards. I was thinking about surprises too, only mine were not good.

WHAT IS NOT EASY

It's not easy to be walking around with a lie hanging over your head. Lies make everything harder. As soon as we got to school, I tried to get away from Mimi so I could work on the card in secret, but that was impossible. Mimi and I went everywhere together, so when I said I needed to go to the library, of course she came with me. "Are you looking for a book?" she asked. I didn't want to lie again, but I had to, at least a little bit—I nodded. Mimi pulled a book off the return cart and looked at it. "What kind of book are you getting?" she asked. I didn't know what to say. I picked some flyers off the library desk and pretended to be reading them. What should I do next? This was a hundred times harder than I thought it was going to be. I shoved the flyers in my backpack and walked toward the door.

"Let's go," I said. Mimi put her book down and followed me. Suddenly Sammy and Max were standing in front of us. "What are you guys doing here?" asked Max. Mimi pointed to me and said, "Grace was looking for a book." I shook my head and mumbled something about changing my mind. Did a lie count less if it was mumbled?

I pushed by Sammy and Max and walked out into the hall. "Hey, you dropped something," said Sammy. I looked down to where he was pointing. It was the flyers from the library—they'd fallen out of my backpack and I didn't need them anymore, so I picked them up and dropped them into the recycling container just outside the library door, and then Mimi and I raced down the hall. The bell was going to ring any second.

THE GOOD THING ABOUT PLANS

If they are not working, you can change them. Now that we were sitting in class I had a new plan: make the card at my desk while Miss Lois was busy talking abut the earth. Drawing a card was going to be a lot easier than trying to figure out if I was hanging upside down.

HOW TO DRAW A CARD AT YOUR DESK

① WHEN MISS LOIS IS LOOKING AT ME I LOOK RIGHT BACK AT HER.

MY DESK IS → CLEAN. THE CARD IS HIDDEN.

② WHEN MISS LOIS IS NOT LOOKING AT ME I DRAW THE CARD.

HOW MISS LOIS RUINED MY PLAN

Instead of teaching us regular stuff like math and spelling like she was supposed to, Miss Lois decided to start the morning with us getting together with our partners. Normally I'd have been super happy about that, but today I wasn't. There was no way to draw a birthday card for Grace F. with Mimi sitting right next to me.

When everyone was in their groups, Miss Lois went to the board and told us what we needed to do for our assignment.

CONTINENT AND OCEAN ASSIGNMENT

1. Find out three facts about your continent or sea.

2. Use at least three sentences to explain each fact.

3. Add a picture or item to go with your fact.

A lot of people were confused by the word item, so Miss Lois had to explain that part some more.

I SHOULD HAVE JUST SAID PICTURES.

WHAT MISS LOIS IS PROBABLY THINKING.

IF YOU WANT, YOU CAN BRING IN AN ITEM INSTEAD OF DRAWING A PICTURE. AN ITEM IS AN ACTUAL PHYSICAL THING. IF ONE OF YOUR FACTS WAS ABOUT GOLD, THEN YOU COULD BRING IN A BAR OF GOLD.

Sometimes when you want things to go super fast, they instead go super slow. This is what was happening today, and it was super annoying. If we didn't finish talking about the earth and get back to our regular work, there'd be no time for me to make a card, not even a bad one. After the second time of explaining everything again, Miss Lois put the names of all the continents and oceans into a plastic bucket. I thought she'd be the chooser, but she said we could do it ourselves. Mimi said I could be the one to pick for our team, probably because I was moving around a lot in my seat. It's hard to be patient and still when you're worried that something bad is about to happen.

I went to the front of the room and stood in line. When it was my turn, I reached into the hat and pulled out South America. I didn't know anything about South America. I waved the slip of paper at Mimi and walked back to my desk. Halfway there, I suddenly stopped.

I was wrong: I did know something about South America. South America had rainforests, and the rainforests were filled with giant bugs! This was not a fun fact to remember.

WHAT YOU WILL DO IF YOU REALLY NEED TO MAKE A CARD

I put my hand up and asked to go to the bathroom. It was the only way I could think of to get away from Mimi. I brought a pen with me, and as soon as I got to the bathroom, I looked around for a piece of paper. Of course that was crazy—there's no real paper in the bathroom. Sometimes even if something is a bad idea, you will still try to make yourself believe it can work out. When something like that happens to you, it's called being desperate.

WHAT FINALLY HAPPENED

I walked back to the class with nothing.

WHAT FEELS TERRIBLE

As soon as the bell rang for lunch, Mimi went back to her own desk to put her stuff away and get the card she'd made for Grace F. I couldn't move. All I could do was sit there and hope to turn invisible. Of course that kind of thing can't happen, so Mimi came over to see why I wasn't getting up. I took a deep breath, ready to tell her everything, but then instead of the truth, out came another lie. "I can't find my card," I said. "It's gone." Mimi looked surprised. She shook her head. "It can't be gone," she said. "We haven't been anywhere—we've been here all morning. Did you look in your backpack?" I got up and she followed me to my locker. Of course I knew it wasn't going to be there, but I pretended to look for it anyway.

As we headed toward the lunchroom, Mimi suddenly grabbed my arm. "I know where it is," she said. She pulled me down the hallway. I had no idea what she was talking about or where we were going, but I followed her until we were standing outside the library in front of the recycling bin. She pointed to it. "Don't you remember? This morning, you threw away some papers. I bet the card was in with those papers." I nodded like I agreed with her, but it was another lie. I did not want to look through the recycling bin to find a card that was not going to be there. It was only paper garbage, but it was still garbage. Mimi looked at her watch and shook her head. I knew what she was thinking. She didn't want to be late for lunch, and because of that I suddenly had an idea.

After Mimi left, I tried to decide what to do. Three minutes wasn't enough time to make a card. There was only one way out—

I'd have to tell the truth. I tried to make myself feel brave. Brave feelings are not easy to find, especially if after being brave you are going to feel embarrassed. Being brave and saying you have been lying is not the same as being brave and climbing a mountain.

Thinking about it made my stomach feel sick. I looked down the hallway to see if I could see Mimi, but I couldn't—she was gone. When I looked back the other way, Mr. Harris, the school principal, was walking toward me. I was hoping he wouldn't notice me, but he stopped right in front of me. Even though Mr. Harris is nice, talking to a principal is still a little bit scary. Principals pretty much notice everything. Mr. Harris looked at me and crinkled up his eyebrows. "Do you feel okay?" he asked. "You look pale—like you've seen a ghost." I knew it was a joke, so I smiled and mumbled that I was okay. He was easy to fool—he didn't know that I was using my pretend smile. He smiled back, nodded, and walked away.

I took a deep breath and looked toward the lunchroom. Everyone was there, and they were waiting for me. If I didn't show up, Mimi would be worried and come looking for me. My feet didn't want to, but I made them move forward. And then suddenly I knew what to say. I had a plan to save myself.

THE GHOST

WHO DID NOT 100 PERCENT BELIEVE ME

Mimi—she was confused. It was easy to tell, because she was looking at me in the exact same way that Mr. Scruffers does when she's confused.

MIMI'S HEAD TO THE SIDE

MR. SCRUFFERS'S HEAD TO THE SIDE

I wanted Mimi to believe me. It was wrong, but I couldn't help it.

WHAT IS HARD

To sit still and pretend to act normal when nothing about what you are doing is normal. It took a while, but finally Mimi said, "Okay." I thought that would be it, but a second later she added another part to her sentence. "After lunch, I want to go and see the ghost." This wasn't good news, but it was better than her not believing me. Plus when we got there, maybe I could just say I'd made a mistake.

WHAT IS VERY HARD TO DO

Keeping lies organized.

While I was worrying about my lies, Grace F. opened all her cards. I said I'd make her a new one, which was 100 percent not a lie. For her party I was going to make the best card I'd ever made. Could an amazing card can-

cel out a big lie? I hoped so. Watching Grace
F. open and read all her cards was not easy.
It made the uncomfortable sick feeling that
was in my stomach come all the way up into
my throat. It was a good thing that no one
could tell that my insides were not matching
up with my outsides.

After lunch we all walked over to the library to look at the recycling bin. It was the

exact thing I did not want to do. I stood behind everyone else and stayed quiet. I didn't want anyone looking at me—sometimes people can tell you are lying just by looking at your face, and I 100 percent did not want that to happen.

"Should I say something?" asked Grace L. I looked at her and shrugged. "Like what?" I asked. Grace L. thought for a minute and then she said, "Well, we could ask it if it's a good ghost or a bad ghost." Grace F. shook her head. "I don't think we should talk to it. It scared Grace so it's probably a bad ghost." Everyone nodded. Now I was feeling guilty in a whole new way.

Mimi crumpled a piece of paper up into a ball and threw it into the recycling bin. I was the only one who wasn't surprised that nothing happened. There was no moaning, no groaning, no anything at all. I tried to explain that maybe I'd made a mistake, but it was too late. No one wanted to believe me—they wanted to believe in the ghost. I didn't know that something like that could happen.

WHAT IS IMPOSSIBLE TO KEEP AS A SECRET

A haunted recycling bin. By the end of the day, everyone knew about it. Now my lie was big and getting bigger by the second. The only way to destroy it was with the truth, and I wasn't brave enough to do that.

WALKING HOME FROM SCHOOL

Mimi and I walked home with Max and Sammy. The only thing Max and Mimi wanted to talk about was the haunted recycling bin. It seemed like the kind of thing Sammy would like, but he was quiet and didn't say anything. Maybe he was scared of ghosts. Maybe ghosts were like cats—things he didn't even want to think about. I made a picture in my head of Sammy battling the recycling bin. It was the first thing all day that made me smile.

I thought people would be scared of the recycling bin, but they weren't—instead they were excited about it and couldn't stop talking about it. Max's big idea was to take a photo of the ghost. He stopped in the middle of the sidewalk and put his hands up. "If we had a picture of the ghost, our school would be famous." I nodded like I thought his idea was the best thing I'd ever heard, but it was another lie. Now I didn't even have to think about the lies—they just happened all on their own. That did not make me feel better.

When we finally got to my house, Mimi went home and I went to get Mr. Scruffers to play in the backyard. After we'd been playing ball for about ten minutes, Augustine Dupre came outside to see us. Her apartment is in our basement so she can see me really easily if I am in the backyard. Most basements aren't very exciting, but ours is different. Our basement has a great apartment in it. I used to go down to the basement all the time, but now that Augustine Dupre is married to Luke, Mom won't let me do that anymore. I'm not allowed to go down there without an invitation. Mom and I have different feelings about it. I call it visiting and Mom calls it bugging, but she is wrong, because when I go downstairs Augustine Dupre is always 100 percent happy to see me.

I threw the ball for Mr. Scruffers, and while she ran off to get it Augustine Dupre walked over to me. "What's new?" she asked. I shrugged my shoulders like there was nothing, but it wasn't true, because the card lie was there hanging over my head, and it was new and very big. For a second I was worried that Augustine Dupre might have superpowers and be able to see it, but after a few seconds I could tell that she didn't. It was invisible.

I'M STILL UP HERE!

GIANT INVISIBLE LIE ABOVE MY HEAD.

WHAT I COULD HAVE SAID TO AUGUSTINE DUPRE IF I WERE BRAVE AND NOT SCARED

I HAVE A PROBLEM. I TOLD A LIE AND NOW I DON'T KNOW HOW TO UNTELL IT.

But I didn't say that—instead I told Augustine Dupre all about the sleepover camping party, and how Dad and I were going to practice in the tent on Friday. Augustine Dupre smiled and said, "Practice makes perfect." I shouldn't have been surprised, but I was, and instantly I was thinking about my lie again. I looked down at the ground. I didn't want Augustine Dupre to see my face. Guilt is not always invisible. Augustine Dupre waited for me to say something, but when I didn't, she smiled and asked if I wanted her and Luke to sneak up on our tent and make spooky noises while we were sleeping. Of course I said no—even Dad would be scared of that.

WHAT DAD BROUGHT HOME FROM WORK

After dinner Dad and I went outside to the car to get the tent. There were two different things in the trunk: a big green bag and a bunch of metal sticks. It wasn't very impressive, but Dad said when we put everything together it would make a fantastic tent. I helped him carry it all out to the backyard. It was hard to imagine how it was going to work. "Don't worry," said Dad, "it'll be easy. If a Boy Scout can do it, so can I." I wanted to put the tent up right away, but Dad said we had to wait until tomorrow, because it was getting dark and I had homework to do. It was disappointing, but I probably deserved it.

WHAT IS HARD TO DO

Fall asleep when you know you've done something wrong. Bad thoughts like to come out at night.

WHAT WAS A SURPRISE

I woke up feeling brave. Today was the day. Today I would tell Mimi the truth. Today I would destroy the lie.

When I got downstairs I asked Mom to make me French toast. French toast is my favorite breakfast to have when I need extra energy. She didn't answer, but I took it as a good sign when she took the frying pan out of the cupboard.

While I was waiting for my French toast, I started thinking about the recycling bin again. Did people really believe that it was haunted? I shook my head. I had a good feeling about today. Probably everyone had forgotten about the recycling can anyway.

WHAT TASTES EXTRA GOOD AFTER YOU HAVE DECIDED THAT EVERYTHING IS GOING TO TURN OUT EXACTLY LIKE YOU WANT IT TO

French toast.

LIE NUMBER ONE

On the way to school I told Mimi how I was really feeling about the sleepover. She was quiet for a minute, and then she pointed at me. "I knew there was something you weren't telling me. I could feel it." I nodded, but didn't say what I was thinking. Mimi did have powers—she'd felt my lies. I knew what was next. Now was the exact right time to tell her everything. I took a deep breath and opened my mouth, but the wrong words came out. Instead of telling her about the card and the recycling bin, I told her about the tent and how Dad was going to help me practice for the party.

WHAT I REALLY WANTED TO ASK MIMI BUT WASN'T BRAVE ENOUGH TO SAY

THE BIG BAD SURPRISE THAT I FOUND OUT ABOUT AS SOON AS A STEPPED ONTO THE PLAYGROUND

Everyone was talking about the haunted recycling bin. And worse than that, other people were even saying that they'd heard strange sounds too. What was happening?

WHAT HAD GOTTEN HUGE

My lie, and now I wasn't the only one feed-
ing it—everyone was. It made me feel dizzy
and sick just thinking about it. Mimi grabbed
my hand and pulled me toward the school.
"Let's go see it. Maybe it looks different."
Most of me wanted to turn right around
and run home and hide, but a little part
of me was curious, so I followed Mimi to the
library. When we got there, a few kids were
pushing each other toward the recycling
bin, but mostly everyone was just standing

back looking at it. "What's it want?" asked a girl. I didn't know her name. "I don't know," answered a boy, and he shrugged. "Well, we should give it whatever it wants to make it go away, because having it there makes me scared to go to the library," said the girl.

Suddenly I was feeling super guilty—my lie was hurting other people. I hadn't thought about that before.

I had to use my empathy super power. It was the exact extra push I needed to feel brave.

I walked over to the recycling bin and put my hand on it. "See, it's okay, the ghost is gone." Suddenly everyone in the hall was quiet. It was more attention than I wanted. The girl shook her head and said, "Well, maybe it's gone now, but it'll come back." I looked around and everyone was nodding. My being brave had changed nothing.

WHAT WAS ANOTHER SURPRISE

That every kid in the whole school was talking about the haunted recycling bin and the teachers didn't even know it existed. The more I thought about it, the more confused I got. What about the people who were saying they'd heard things—were they making it up? Why would they do that?

I was glad that Miss Lois was keeping us busy. I didn't want to think about it anymore. We spent the morning learning about land formations. There were a lot of them I didn't know. Miss Lois had us each pick out five and write about them in our earth books. A lot of the boys picked butte—it wasn't funny and had nothing to do with what they were thinking, but boys are weird that way.

BUTTE

Miss Lois said we could be creative with our land formations, so I made mine into a sideways face. It was a nice way to keep my brain busy. A busy brain is a good thing, because a busy brain doesn't have time to worry.

SIDE DRAWING OF A FACE
WITH LAND FORMATIONS

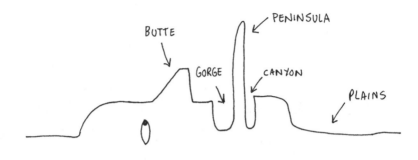

LUNCHTIME

When I saw Max walking toward Mimi and me in the lunchroom, I knew something was going on. We are friends after school, but we don't usually talk at lunchtime. Max stood right in front of us and pointed to the door. "It's gone," he said. I had no idea what he was talking about. "What's gone?" asked Mimi. "The recycling bin," said Max. "They took it away. The people that clean the school, they got rid of it." I almost choked on my sandwich. I couldn't believe what he was saying. It was the most surprising fantastic news ever. Max looked at me. "Why are you smiling?" he asked. This time I didn't have to lie. "Because the ghost is gone," I said. Max shook his head. "I kind of liked the ghost," he said. Now I shook my head. I wasn't even going to pretend to agree with him, because he was wrong. The ghost being gone was great!

The rest of the afternoon went by super fast, and even though it was just spelling and math, I loved it.

WHAT WAS WAITING FOR ME IN THE BACKYARD WHEN I GOT HOME

Dad, Mr. Scruffers, and the tent. Dad had some of the poles put together, but he was waiting for me to help him with the hard parts. I'm lucky that Dad's good at following directions, because putting the tent together was not easy. I thought we'd be done in about ten minutes, but it took forever. It wasn't as big as I thought it was going to be, but Dad said there was room for all of us, even Mom if she wanted to sleep outside too. At dinner Dad asked her about it, but I knew what she was going to say, and I was right. She said no. I was secretly glad about that. Mom in a tent seemed like a bad idea. When Mom's not happy, she likes to do a lot of complaining.

Knowing that Dad was going to sleep in the tent with me tomorrow made me feel a lot better. I didn't have one single bad thought all night long. And for the first time ever, I smiled when I thought about the recycling bin—someone out there was my hero.

HERO

PERSON THAT HELPS CLEAN THE SCHOOL →

WOW! I DIDN'T KNOW CUSTODIANS COULD GET MEDALS AND CROWNS.

THE BAD SURPRISE AT SCHOOL IN THE MORNING

THE RECYCLING BIN WAS BACK! It wasn't thrown away—it was just moved. Now instead of it being outside the library, it was in the hall beside the gym. Max was the one who told us. As soon as Mimi and I stepped onto the playground, he ran over and gave us the news. At first Mimi didn't believe him. She put her hands on her hips like moms do when they are mad at their kids. "How can you tell it's the same one?" she asked. "All the recycling containers look the same." It was a good question. I crossed my fingers and hoped that Max didn't have a good answer. He grinned at Mimi. That made me wor-

ried. People with wrong or bad answers do not grin. "The containers all have numbers on them," said Max. "And the one with the ghost is number zero-eight-three, plus two people already heard it moaning." I uncrossed my fingers. Suddenly I wanted to moan too.

The bell rang just as Max was walking away, so Mimi and I didn't have time to go and look at container 083. I was glad about that. I didn't want to see it. Just thinking about it made me feel bad.

WHAT HAPPENED AT LUNCHTIME

Of course Mimi and I had to go and look for the recycling container, but when we went to the gym, it was gone. I was happy for about ten minutes, but then right before lunchtime someone found it outside the art room. Who was moving it around so much? And why? It was making things worse. Now it was like a game: everyone wanted to find it.

WHAT HAPPENED ON THE WAY HOME

Mimi had to go to the dentist after school, so I walked home with Sammy and Max. It wasn't the best walk home, because Max was the only one talking. Both Sammy and I hardly said a word.

When we got to my house Sammy asked if Crinkles was around. That wasn't a usual thing for Sammy to ask about. He hates cats. I didn't know how to answer, partly because I was surprised by the question, and partly because I didn't know the answer. Crinkles is not my cat. He belongs to Mrs. Luther, my next-door neighbor, so he could be any-where. Cats are not like dogs—they like to hide. Finally I just looked around the yard and said, "No, he's not here." That seemed to make Sammy a lot happier. He half smiled at Max and said, "See you tomorrow." Max waved and we both watched him walk down the street.

I didn't know what to say, so Sammy and I just stood there, not saying anything. It felt weird, but that's how things with Sammy usu-ally are—unusual and uncomfortable. He's not an easy person to figure out. As soon as Max turned the corner and was gone, Sammy turned to me and said, "You have to do something about the recycling container. If you don't, Mr. Woods is going to get in trouble." Then Sammy shook his head. "And you might too." I was shocked. I couldn't speak. What did he know? What did he mean? Who was Mr. Woods? Sammy shook his head again, and then he told me everything.

WHAT IS HARD

To not cry when someone has just told you that he knows you are big fat liar, even if when he said it he didn't use those exact words. My whole face was red. I could feel it. I put my head down.

SAMMY'S IDEA

SOMETIMES IN ANCIENT TIMES PEOPLE USED TO GIVE GHOSTS AND SPIRITS OFFERINGS TO MAKE THEM GO AWAY.

MAYBE YOU COULD SAY YOU DID THAT, AND NOW THE GHOST IS HAPPY SO IT'S GONE.

THAT WAY YOU WOULDN'T HAVE TO SAY YOU MADE THE WHOLE THING UP.

SAMMY STILL LOOKING DOWN

WHAT IS STRANGE

How sometimes you can be completely surprised by a good idea, especially if it comes from someone who you do not think of as a good idea kind of person.

After Sammy finished explaining everything, I forced myself to talk. "I'll do something," I said. I still couldn't look at his face, so I stared down at the grass. I saw Sammy's feet move away, so I took a chance and looked up. He smiled. It wasn't a you're-in-trouble smile. Instead it was an I'm-glad-this-is-over smile.

If I could have, I would have smiled back, because I was feeling exactly the same way, but I couldn't. My body was still too shocked and embarrassed for smiling. I couldn't wait for Sammy to leave. The minute he started walking away, I was gone. I didn't even stop to pet Mr. Scruffers—I just ran straight up to

my room, closed the door and flopped down
on my bed.

WHAT MY BRAIN WAS THINKING

1. Why didn't Sammy tell on me?
2. Does he think I'm an awful person?
3. How does he know Mr. Woods?
4. Does Mr. Woods think I'm an awful person?
5. Could Sammy's plan work to make the
   pretend ghost go away?

WAITING
FOR THE
IDEAS.

Sometimes thinking can be hard. Sometimes you need help. I went to my closet and pulled out my Super Girl T-shirt. I put it on and waited for my brain to fill up with ideas.

Waiting can be more fun if you are not doing it alone. I opened the door and let Mr. Scruffers in. She was happy about that. It was a lot better than standing outside in the hall whining.

The only thing I could think of was that even with everything bad happening, I was still kind of lucky—lucky to have a friend like Sammy.

DISAPPOINTING, BUT TRUE

Even if you want a great idea and are really ready for it, it doesn't mean you are going to get one. When Mom called me down for dinner, I still didn't have an idea. It's hard to eat food when your body is filled with worry.

WHAT HELPED ME FEEL ABOUT 85 PERCENT BETTER EVEN THOUGH IT DID NOT SOLVE MY PROBLEM

Talking with Dad about sleeping in the tent.

I had completely forgotten that tonight was the night for sleeping outside. I guess worry can do that, too.

THE ONLY BAD THING ABOUT SLEEPING IN A TENT

I wasn't going to get to flash my lights for Mimi. Suddenly, just after thinking that, I had

a great idea, but it wasn't the great idea I was hoping for. It was a different one.

MIMI, LOOK OUTSIDE YOUR WINDOW AT NINE O'CLOCK. I'LL BE IN MY YARD AND I'LL FLASH MY FLASHLIGHT THREE TIMES FOR YOU.

Me and Dad. It was great, and not even one bit scary like I thought it was going to be. Dad told me some great stories from when he was a boy. My favorite was about the time he stole a bouncy ball by accident. It made me laugh, and then also think that maybe Dad and I were kind of the same when it came to worrying.

I told Dad that is was silly for him to bury the ball. At first he agreed with me, but then he said that burying the ball had helped him feel better. Dad said, "Sometimes it's hard to get over something just by thinking about it. Sometimes it's easier if your body can do something physical to help your brain." I nodded like I understood, but I only kind of got it.

WHO DID NOT LIKE SLEEPING IN THE TENT

Mr. Scruffers. Every time Dad or I even moved an inch, she jumped up and whined at the zipper door, asking to be let out. The first couple of times it was funny and cute, but then after a while it was annoying. Finally we just had to put her in the house with Mom. I was a little sad about that, but Mom was probably happy to have the company. She said she was going to let Mr. Scruffers sleep in Dad's spot on the bed as a special treat.

I'M SORRY, I'M JUST NOT A CAMPING DOG.

STANDING ON DAD'S PILLOW.

THE FOUR BEST THINGS ABOUT SLEEPING OUTSIDE

1. Flashing my lights at Mimi with the flashlight.
2. Standing outside in the dark and looking up at the stars.
3. How quiet everything is at night, and how the noises that you do hear are not scary like I thought they would be.
4. Waking up early and smelling the day. Dad said it was probably the flowers in the yard, but I had never noticed that smell before. The day smelled good!

THE SURPRISING THING ABOUT SLEEPING OUTSIDE

We got up a lot earlier than normal. Mom and Mr. Scruffers were still sleeping when we went inside. Dad made us toast and scrambled eggs, and as soon as he started cooking, Mr. Scruffers came running in. She was super excited to see me, like she thought I'd been gone far away for the whole night. Some things are too hard to explain to a dog, so I just gave her lots of attention and pretended she was right.

And then, right when I was petting Mr. Scruffers and not thinking at all about my ghost problem, I suddenly had an idea. One second my brain was normal, and the next second, like magic, there it was—full of an idea. Sometimes you can figure out exactly where an idea comes from. This was one of those times.

MY NEW IDEA

DO SOMETHING

BE NICE

THIS PART FROM DAD'S BALL STORY.

THIS PART FROM BEING EXTRA NICE TO MR. SCRUFFERS.

THE MORNING

Mimi came over extra early this morning, and I knew exactly why—she wanted to know how I'd liked sleeping in the tent. When I told her it was great, she jumped up and down and clapped her hands. "I was worried you wouldn't like it and wouldn't want to stay for the sleepover part," she said. I nodded. I'd been thinking about that too, but now that worry was gone. While Dad made Mimi some scrambled eggs, I told her about my idea for the recycling bin.

After I told her the idea, Mimi was quiet for a minute, but then she smiled. It was a good sign that she liked the idea too.

WHAT HAPPENED AFTER BREAKFAST THAT WAS UNUSUAL

I told Mimi that I needed to be alone so I could work on a birthday card for Grace. Usually Mimi and I spend as much time as we can together, but today was different.

After Mimi left I helped Dad take down the tent. It was a lot faster to put away than it was to put up. Dad said that was the way most things were, harder to build than to destroy. Right away my brain thought of one example where that was wrong, but I didn't tell him about it.

THE CARD FOR GRACE F.

Amazing cards take a long time to make. I worked on the card until it was almost time to go to the party. I don't know if it was going to make up for not giving her one when everyone else did, but it was a really good try.

THREE CARDS IN ONE

THE PARTY

Dad drove Mimi and me to the party on his way to give back the tent to his friend. Once Mimi and I got everything into the car, it was pretty full. Pillows, sleeping bags, favorite stuffed animals, clothes—all that stuff takes up a lot of room. Grace L., Marta, and the girl named Lisa were already at Grace F.'s house when we got there. Right away I could tell that I was going to like the new girl. I don't know why it happens that way, but sometimes you can just tell that about people.

Grace F. is a very organized person. As soon as we walked in the door she picked up a checklist and asked us if we had all the stuff we needed. She said it was so we wouldn't have to call our parents to bring over stuff we had forgotten, but that probably wasn't 100 percent true. I think it was mostly because she just loves making lists.

After we passed the checklist, we all went outside to look at the tent and put our sleeping stuff in it. Grace F. wanted everyone to see the tent all at once, because when something is amazing you want to save it for a big ta-da moment. And Grace F.'s tent was worth it! It was not like a normal tent—it was beautiful. The outside was covered with tiny lights, and inside there were colored pillows, a real carpet, and even a chandelier. Grace F. said the chandelier was a birthday present from her grandma and it worked with batteries so you could put it anywhere. It was one of those things that I didn't know existed, but now that I did, I wanted one too. Suddenly I was super excited about the tent. This wasn't normal camping like I'd done with Dad—this was fancy camping!

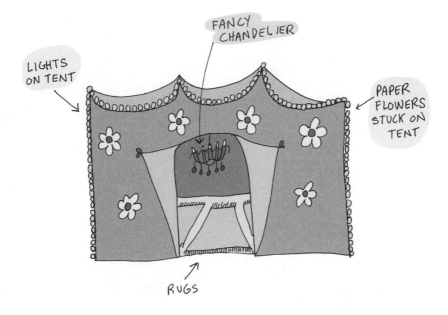

I looked over at Grace L. to see if she seemed sad—but she didn't, she looked normal. I don't know how her brain could not be wishing she could stay overnight.

The first thing we did was go back inside to make the stuffed creatures Mimi had told me about. Grace F. has a pretty big house, so she and her mom have one whole room just for art stuff. It's kind of like an art lover's dream come true.

THE STUFFED CREATURE WE ARE DECORATING

GOOGLY EYES

FELT THAT HAS A STICKY BACK

All SORTS OF GLITTER GLUE

MARKERS

GLITTER

THE GOOD THING ABOUT A CRAFT WITH GLUE

Crafts with glue get finished a lot faster than crafts that you have to sew. Everyone except

Mimi used glue to decorate their stuffed creature, and when we all went outside to jump on the trampoline, Mimi was still sewing. I asked if she wanted me to stay with her, but she shook her head. When Mimi is sewing her hands and her whole body are happy. It's hard to stop doing something that you love that much, even for trampoline jumping.

When we came back inside for water, Mimi was just finishing up her stuffed creature. It was perfect timing, because the glue on our creatures was finally dry too. Grace F.'s mom had pizza for us, but before she let us eat anything we had to pose for a bunch of pictures while holding our creatures. She must like photography a lot, because she took about a hundred photos. It's not easy to concentrate on smiling for so long when your stomach is growling and your nose smells pizza.

WHAT I DIDN'T KNOW

Pizza tastes better when you eat it on a trampoline. I've probably had pizza about a million times, but the pizza we had at Grace F.'s party was the most delicious pizza I'd ever had, and I wasn't the only one thinking that. When we were done eating, Lisa invented a new game for us to play. It was called Crust-out. No one ate their pizza crusts, so we dumped them all into the middle of the trampoline, and then when Lisa said *go,* we jumped around and tried to not let them touch us. If a pizza crust touched you, even just your toe, you were out.

I've never done so much screaming in my whole life. It was so fun! I didn't win the game, but that didn't matter—no one really cared about the winning part anyway. Now I had another new thing for my list.

THINGS THAT I WANT LIST

1. CHANDELIER
2. TRAMPOLINE

WHAT IS NOT SO FUN

Having to clean up the pizza crusts when we were done playing the game. Grace F.'s mom was not like us. She didn't think that pizza crusts bouncing around on the trampoline was a good idea.

After everything was cleaned up, Grace F.'s mom and sister Stephanie came out to hang up the big sheet for the movie. Grace F. wouldn't say what movie we were going to watch, but I already knew. She'd told Mimi about it a few days ago, and then Mimi had told me. I don't think Mimi knew it was supposed to be a secret, because all of a sudden she looked at me and shook her head. I knew exactly what she was meaning, so I nodded back at her. Sometimes best friends don't need words to talk to each other.

Mimi's head shake = "Don't tell Grace F. I told you what the movie is."
My nod back = "Don't worry, I won't say a thing."

WHAT STEPHANIE WAS

Super nice! Sometimes older kids can be sort of scary and grumpy, but Grace F.'s older sister was nothing like that. She didn't look anything like Grace F. either. Her hair was short, and she was super tall. After she finished helping her mom put up the giant sheet for the movie screen, she came over and said hi to us all.

WHAT IS A GOOD WAY TO GET YOUR YOUNGER SISTER'S FRIENDS TO INSTANTLY LIKE YOU

THE MOVIE

I was hoping that we would get to watch the movie from the trampoline, but we couldn't, because the only place to hang up the big screen was on the garage, and that was at the back of the house near the tent. Pretty much everyone except Grace L. had seen the movie before, but that was okay, because it was a good movie and no one minded watching it again. Plus it was about being at camp, so it was perfect for a camping sleepover. The only bad part was that we had to keep telling Marta to shush, because she is one of those people who like to talk during a movie and tell you what is going to happen next. Even if you've seen the movie before, that kind of thing can be annoying. And if you haven't seen the movie before, it can totally ruin it for you.

Stephanie finally came up with a great way to keep Marta quiet. She sat beside her and every time Marta opened her mouth to talk, she offered her another taffy candy. It was Marta's favorite candy, and it worked perfectly to keep her mouth busy. It's hard to eat sticky candy and talk at the same time.

After the movie Grace F.'s dad came out and started a fire so we could make s'mores. The fire was nice, but hardly anyone was hungry. We were all too full.

I CAN'T EAT ANYTHING S'MORE.

WHAT I WAS SURPRISED ABOUT

That there wasn't a birthday cake, or even birthday cupcakes. Grace F. said that instead, we were going to have a birthday pancake cake for breakfast in the morning. I had no idea what a birthday pancake was, but it was a relief not to have to stuff down a piece of birthday cake.

WHAT I DON'T HAVE TO SAY

Grace L. left after the movie, but she said she was sad about missing the pancake birthday cake, so her mom promised to bring her back in the morning. Grace L. didn't say why she was going home, but after she left Marta said, "Grace L. only likes to sleep in her own bed." Her saying that made me suddenly miss Mr. Scruffers and wonder where she was going to sleep. Dad said, *No dogs on my bed,* but after he'd said that Mom had winked at me. Dad didn't know it, but Mom's wink was probably stronger than his no.

MR. SCRUFFERS SLEEPING AT THE END OF MOM AND DAD'S BED.

THIS IS NICE, BUT THE PILLOW IS BETTER.

WHAT I HAD NEVER DONE BEFORE

Heard a spooky story while sitting around a fire. Grace F.'s dad said he didn't think a spooky story was a good idea, but when he went to the bathroom Stephanie told us one anyway.

THIS IS THE STORY OF THE RACCOOBAT. IT LIVES AROUND HERE SO WE HAVE TO BE CAREFUL.

IT ONLY COMES OUT AT NIGHT IF YOU CALL IT BY MAKING THIS STRANGE SOUND— SNORT, SNORT, SNORT!

NO ONE KNOWS WHAT IT EATS, BUT SOME PEOPLE THINK IT LIKES SNACKS JUST LIKE THE ONES WE HAVE HERE.

It was more funny than scary, because we all knew that she was making it up. There's no such thing as a raccoobat, and the snorting noises she made were really funny.

When we finally went into the tent I was pretty sleepy. Grace F. had been saving her birthday presents for bedtime, so the first thing she wanted to do was open them. I usually love watching people open their presents, but this time it was hard to stay awake. She got jewelry, fun clothes, and lots of art supplies. She was super excited about the art supplies—Grace F. loves art. When she got to my card she looked at it for a long time, and then said thank you. Right away I knew one thing—her thank-you was real.

The only present she didn't open was the present from Grace L. She said she was going to wait until Grace came back in the morning. That was a nice thing to do. It's not easy to resist opening a present.

THE LIST

My eyes were having a really hard time staying open, but before Stephanie let anyone go to sleep she gave us each a flashlight and read us three rules. It was easy to promise to do everything on the list, which was good, because I could tell that she was serious about it.

1. DON'T LEAVE THE YARD FOR ANY REASON.

2. IF YOU HAVE TO GO TO THE BATHROOM, WAKE ME UP BUT BE WARNED, I WILL BE GRUMPY!

3. THE ONLY OTHER REASON TO WAKE ME UP IS AN EMERGENCY.
AN EMERGENCY IS...
WILD ANIMAL, FIRE, ACCIDENT, ALIENS, FLOOD.

STEPHANIE'S LIST

WHAT FEELS AMAZING

Putting your head down on your very own pillow when you are super tired. We all talked for a while, but I don't remember what we were talking about. I wasn't paying very much attention. Mimi said she was still going to try to wake up in the middle of the night to look at the stars, but I had a feeling that wasn't going to happen. When your body is super tired, it's not easy to wake up in the middle of sleeping.

WHAT I WAS NOT SCARED OF, EVEN THOUGH I THOUGHT ABOUT THEM FOR A FEW SECONDS

Beetles.

WHAT WAS A SURPRISE IN THE MIDDLE OF THE NIGHT

Mimi shaking me, but it wasn't because she wanted to look at the stars. It was because she, and everyone else in the tent, was scared of the raccoobat!

"She's calling the raccoobat," whispered Grace F. "What if it comes?" whispered Lisa. I shook my head. "There's no such thing. She made it up." Everyone nodded and agreed with me, but still it didn't matter. In the middle of the night, things that you know are not true can suddenly seem true. Hearing Stephanie make that sound was definitely scary. "Let's wake her up and make her stop," said Marta. "Or we could just poke her," said Mimi. Mimi put out her hand, but Grace F. grabbed it away. "We can't wake her up," she said. "It'll be worse than the raccoobat. She'll be mad. Remember the list?" Everyone was quiet for a minute, thinking about the list. Grace F. was right. We had promised. "But maybe this is an emergency?" whispered Marta. We all shook our heads. It wasn't one of the emergencies from the list. Suddenly I had an idea. It didn't break any of Stephanie's rules, and it got us away from Stephanie and the raccoobat.

LET'S GO AND SLEEP ON THE TRAMPOLINE.

At first no one liked my idea, but after Stephanie made three more raccoobat sounds, everyone agreed to do it. The only hard part about getting out of the tent was walking through all the piles of papers from the presents. We finally pushed them to the side so no one would trip.

WHAT WAS AMAZING

Lying on the trampoline all cozy in my sleeping bag looking up at the stars. Mimi said it was perfect, and much better than just standing outside looking up at the sky. We set up our flashlights all around us, and then huddled together in the middle of the trampoline. I was glad about two things.

1. That Dad had helped me be not scared of camping.

2. That the trampoline had a net around it.

  Thinking glad thoughts and looking up at the stars is a good way to fall asleep.

WHAT ARE BAD SOUNDS TO WAKE UP TO

SCREAMING AND YELLING!

When we first heard the screaming we were really scared, but then after a few seconds, we couldn't help it—we all had to laugh.

WHAT STOPS A PERSON FROM SCREAMING

Hearing people laugh. As soon as she heard us, Stephanie came running around the corner to the trampoline. At first she was really mad, but then when she finally believed that we hadn't done it on purpose to scare her, she sort of forgave us. She said she would forgive us 100 percent if we were quiet about it and didn't tell Grace F.'s mom and dad what had happened.

She was lucky that we were fast at promising, because two seconds later both her mom and dad came running out of the house to see what was going on. "Just fun on the trampoline," said Stephanie. "Well, you should know better than to let everyone be screaming so loud at six o'clock in the morning!" said Grace F.'s mom. She had her hands on her hips. I snuck a look at everyone standing next to me, and we all had our heads down. It's no fun to get yelled at, especially when you don't deserve it. After the parents left, Stephanie promised to paint all our nails as a special thank-you. Grace F. was super excited about that. "Wait until you see how good she is," she said. "She can even draw little pictures."

While we waited for Grace F.'s mom to make the birthday pancake, Stephanie painted our nails. Grace F. was right—she was really good at it.

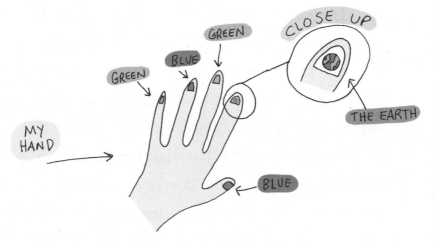

Grace L. came back for breakfast, and even though Grace L. wasn't there for the promise, Stephanie still painted her nails too. Everything that was happening made me feel happy that I had Mimi as a best friend, because if I didn't, I'd definitely be adding another thing to

IT WOULD BE FUN TO HAVE A SISTER.

my list, and it was something Mom and Dad were probably never going to get me.

THE BIRTHDAY PANCAKE CAKE

When something is amazing and your tongue has never tasted it before, it is hard to talk, and when you do finally talk, all your mouth can say is stuff like "Mmmm, mmmmm, mmm-mmmm!"

BIRTHDAY PANCAKE CAKE

CANDLES GO UP HERE

TOP HAS SPRINKLED SUGAR AND WHIPPED CREAM

STRAWBERRIES
WHIPPED CREAM
STRAWBERRIES
CHOCOLATE SAUCE

After breakfast we all went to jump on the trampoline again. That was a good idea for most of us, except for Grace L. She said jumping around after eating the pancake was making her feel sick. When she got off the trampoline I didn't pay any attention to where she went, but about two minutes later, we heard her scream-ing. Of course we all went running to find her. She was

inside the tent, squished up against the back wall, and right in between her and us was a small beetle.

I am definitely not a beetle person, but for some reason, even though it was Grace L. screaming and saying *help me,* I felt sorry for the beetle. It was almost like it was say-ing *help me* too. Suddenly my empathy power was working. I had to save the beetle before someone squished or stepped on it. Without thinking, I grabbed an empty plastic cup left over from the party, ran into the tent, and scooped the beetle into it. Everyone was surprised—even me!

WHAT I DID WITH THE BEETLE

Just because you save a beetle doesn't mean you want to keep a beetle. I was going to put it in the bushes, but Mimi asked if she could have it. "I'll take it home as a surprise for Robert," she said. "He can keep it for a day, and then we'll let it go tonight." I nodded and gave Mimi the cup. Robert was lucky—she was a good sister.

WHAT MIMI SAID THAT SURPISED ME

Mimi, the beetle, and I were all sitting on Grace F.'s front steps waiting for Mimi's mom to come and get us. Except for us, Lisa was the last person to leave. It was sad to think that we weren't going to see her again, so Grace F. promised to invite Lisa, Mimi, and me over again really soon. I was glad about that, because when you meet someone you like, it's kind of weird to say goodbye forever.

After Lisa left, Grace F. went inside to get something. As soon as she was gone Mimi said, "You were really brave." At first I was confused. "About the beetle?" I asked. Mimi shook her head. "Sure," said Mimi, "but mostly I meant about the raccoobat." I nodded. It was nice to have a compliment that I didn't have to try to give back. I don't know why, but it suddenly made me think about Augustine Dupre's saying again—*Practice makes perfect*. Maybe it was time to practice being brave.

WHAT I WAS GLAD ABOUT

That I didn't have to do anything for the whole rest of the day except play with Mr. Scruffers and then rest. Sleepovers can be exhausting.

BEING BRAVE

The next morning when I got up I decided that as soon as I saw Mimi, I was going to tell her everything. I was going to tell her about the card and the lie, and then ask her a million times to forgive me.

WHAT I TOLD MIMI WHEN I SAW HER ON THE WAY TO SCHOOL

I told her that today I was going to start getting rid of the ghost by using the good deeds idea. It would have been better to tell her the truth—that there wasn't a ghost—but being brave is not as easy as I thought it would be. I needed to practice more.

WHAT KIDS ARE GOOD AT

Kids are great about spreading information, and they can do it much faster than teachers. Kids don't need to hand out flyers for everyone to know what is going on. But I made one up just in case. This time it was easy for me to draw in secret, mostly because the secret was only from one person, Miss Lois. Keeping a secret from Miss Lois was a lot easier than keeping a secret from both Mimi and Miss Lois. I can listen and draw at the same time, so I wasn't completely ignoring Miss Lois. I got a lot done this morning—I learned about the Northern Hemisphere, the Southern Hemisphere, the Eastern Hemisphere, the Western Hemisphere, the equator, and how to

HELP MAKE THE GHOST LEAVE

GHOST BE GONE

GOOD IS STRONGER THAN BAD

1. DO A GOOD DEED
2. WRITE IT DOWN
3. THROW IT IN HERE

use a compass, and I also made twelve flyers. If Miss Lois had known she would have been mad but also probably a little bit impressed too.

WHAT WAS HARD

It was hard to wait for lunch. Both Mimi and I couldn't wait to do a good deed and then throw the paper into the recycling bin. Mimi wanted to see if it would make the ghost go away, and I wanted to see if it would make people think the ghost went away. They were kind of the same thing, but different, too. As soon as the bell rang, we ran out into the hall and Mimi helped me give out the flyers. I thought people might have lots of questions, but it was not like when Miss Lois handed out an assignment—no one said anything.

After the flyers were handed out, Mimi and I looked around for some good deed opportunities. It wasn't as easy as I thought it would be. Mimi picked up a candy wrapper off the floor and threw that away, but I couldn't find anything. I was just about to give up when I saw Mr. Harris's secretary, Mrs. W., walking down the hall. Mrs. W. probably does other stuff, but her main job is to sit outside Mr. Harris's office and stare at you while you wait for him to be able to see you. She is very good at that job, and her eyes can make your body feel very nervous.

Mrs. W. was carrying a huge stack of paper and about five or six boxes of markers. She looked like she was having trouble, so I ran over and helped her with the markers. It's not something I would usually do, but I really needed to do a good deed, and she needed help. I guess she thought it was unusual, too, because she looked really surprised. People probably didn't help her very often. When part of your job is making kids feel nervous, you're not a very popular person. I carried the markers for her all the way to the art room, which was perfect, because that's exactly where the recycling container was.

For the whole way down there neither one of us said anything. Mrs. W. wasn't a talking kind of person, and I couldn't think of anything to say. Mimi followed behind us, but she didn't say anything either. The only two words that Mrs. W. said were *thank you,* and that was after I put the markers on the counter in the art room. I looked up to see if she was giving me her evil eye, but she wasn't— she was smiling. I'd never seen her smile before. It made her eyes kind of sparkly and less scary-looking. I gave her a smile back, and

then I went out to the hall to find Mimi. It's funny, but a little thing like a smile can kind of change the whole way you think about someone.

GHOST BE GONE

Mimi was waiting for me by the recycling container. She had two scraps of paper and two pencils ready. She gave me a pencil and paper, and we each wrote out our good deeds. "You go first," said Mimi. She pointed to the recycling container. "Yours is better than mine." I nodded, took a few steps forward, threw in my good deed, and then stepped back so Mimi could do hers. We waited for a few seconds, both watching the recycling bin to see if anything would happen, but, of course, nothing did. I don't know why, but I suddenly had a strange feeling about this whole thing, and not the strange feeling I'd had before. This was a new one.

When we got to the lunchroom, everyone wanted to know why we were so late. All
Mimi said was "good deeds," and instantly
everyone knew what we were talking about.
It was kind of exciting. I had a feeling that
more good deeds were going to get done in
our school today than ever before in history.

After we'd finished eating, Mimi wanted
to go back to the art room to check on the
recycling container. I was glad that she didn't
want to do another good deed. I had the feeling that good deeds were not going to be very
easy to find anymore. When we got there,

there was a line of kids waiting for their turns to throw pieces of paper into the recycling bin. I know I shouldn't have, but I felt kind of proud to have started so many people doing good deeds. I looked over at Mimi. She was smiling too. "I think it's going to work," she said. I nodded. I was almost too shocked to speak.

WHAT SAMMY SAID TO ME IN CLASS

Nothing, but he smiled and nodded. And I was pretty sure I knew what that meant. This time I wasn't too embarrassed to smile back at him.

THE SURPRISING FUN THING WE DID IN THE AFTERNOON

Sometimes even if you know someone, they can still surprise you. Miss Lois was being like that about our earth project. Ever since we started it, she had stopped acting like her normal self. Suddenly she was a lot more fun and filled with surprises. If anyone wanted an answer as to why, I knew what it was. It was love.

Miss Lois had everyone get together with our earth partners, and then she split us up into three groups. Mimi and I got picked for group one. At first I wasn't sure if I should be happy about that, but when Miss Lois said, "Okay, group one, follow me outside," I knew it was good. Groups two and three didn't get to go outside. Instead they had to go to the library to do research on their assignments.

When we got outside, Miss Lois gave each partner team a compass and a list of instructions. Then she took us to a special starting point and told us to use the compass and the instructions to find our treasure. Even though we all knew that the treasure was only going to be a piece of pa-

per, it was still exciting. And it was even more exciting when she said that the first team back with the treasure would get a special prize.

OUR
INSTRUCTIONS

WALK 16 STEPS N
WALK 5 STEPS E
WALK 7 STEPS NW
WALK 10 STEPS S
WALK 15 STEPS SW
WALK 10 STEPS S
LOOK FOR YOUR
TREASURE.

WHAT WAS LUCKY

It was lucky that Mimi was not like me and drawing flyers when Miss Lois was teaching the class about how to use the compass. She had been paying 100 percent attention, and she knew exactly how to use it. I gave her the compass and I took the instructions. At first I thought everyone would be rushing off to the same place, but it didn't work that way— all of our instructions were different. That was good and bad. Good because there was no cheating by just following someone else, but bad because we couldn't tell if we were winning or not.

Mimi was fantastic with the compass. She said the only tricky part was holding it still. When we finished the last clue, we were standing right in front of a tree. Mimi saw the paper before I did. It was just above our heads wrapped around a branch. She pulled it off and we raced back to where Miss Lois was standing. As soon as we started running I knew that we were not going to win. There were two other teams running back too, and they were closer to Miss Lois than we were. We tried to run faster, but we couldn't beat them. We came in third place.

When we handed in our treasure paper, Miss Lois told us that she had changed her mind. "Everyone who finishes can have a treat," she said. This was great news, and almost everyone was happy about it.

After the treasure hunt Miss Lois made us all promise two things:

1. We would not tell the other teams about what we had done until everyone had had their turn.

2. We would work quietly on our projects in the library.

Mostly we had to promise the last thing because Miss Lois knew that some kids get wild and crazy after they eat candy, and she didn't want to get in trouble from the librarian.

WHAT WAS NOT HARD AND SURPRISINGLY KIND OF FUN

Keeping the promises to Miss Lois. Sometimes it's fun to have a secret, especially if it is not the kind of secret that is going to get you into trouble.

The research stuff was pretty easy. Mimi's fact was that South America has the world's largest rainforest and it is home to more than two and a half MILLION different kinds of bugs. After she told me that, I was pretty sure about one thing.

My fact was that South America has the world's highest waterfall. It's called Santo Del

Angel Falls and is 3,212 feet high. That's taller than three Eiffel Towers standing together on top of each other. It's pretty had to imagine what that would look like. It almost made me want to go to South America to see it, but then I remembered the bugs. If millions of bugs stood on each other's shoulders they'd be pretty tall too, and that many bugs I did not want to see.

Our last fact was that the Andes mountain range is more than four thousand miles long. That's a lot of mountains.

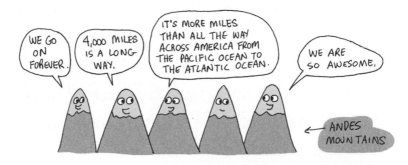

Speech bubbles:
WE GO ON FOREVER.

4,000 MILES IS A LONG WAY.

IT'S MORE MILES THAN ALL THE WAY ACROSS AMERICA FROM THE PACIFIC OCEAN TO THE ATLANTIC OCEAN.

WE ARE SO AWESOME.

← ANDES MOUNTAINS

WHAT I WAS SURPRISED TO FIND OUT

After school Mimi and I went to go and look at the recycling bin outside the art room, but we couldn't find it—it was gone. There was a recycling bin there, but it was the wrong one—the number on the side was not 083, but was 054. Right away Mimi wanted to walk around the school and look for the missing one. I was hoping it would be gone for good, but we found it outside the teachers' lunchroom. Mr. Woods was tricky in moving it around, but he wasn't tricky enough. If we could find it, other kids would too.

WHAT IS NOT VERY EXCITING

Staring at a recycling container when nothing is happening. After a few minutes of looking, we decided to go home. Mimi was going to come over and work with me on our earth project, but she was going to wait until I had played with Mr. Scruffers first. Mimi likes calm dogs much better than excited dogs.

HOW MR. SCRUFFERS IS WHEN I FIRST GET HOME.

HOW MR. SCRUFFERS IS AFTER I PLAY WITH HER FOR TWENTY MINUTES.

GOING CRAZY WITH EXCITEMENT

NICE AND CALM

EARTH PRESENTATIONS

For our earth projects Miss Lois wanted us to write out the facts in nice sentences and add pictures. Some kids complained about that, but Mimi and I like projects. I drew a picture of the world's largest waterfall and Mimi drew a picture of the Andes Mountains. When we got to the Amazon forest part of the project, Mimi surprised me. Sometimes even if you aren't crazy about an idea you can still agree to do it.

I'm good at making fancy letters, so Mimi said I should be the one to write the title of our project on our board.

WHAT LOOKED REALLY GREAT FOR ABOUT TWO SECONDS, UNTIL I NOTICED THE HUGE MISTAKE

THREE GREAT FATS ABOUT SOUTH AMERICA

I had spelled the word *facts* wrong! It was a disaster because everything else was already stuck on the board.

It's not a good feeling to be excited and proud about something and then find out the next second that you made a huge mistake. The only lucky part of the whole thing was that Mimi was not mad about it. Mimi is more of a problem solver than a get-mad-because-there-is-a-problem type of person. She looked at it for a second and scrunched up her nose. "Glue a piece of paper on top of the mistake," she said. That was all it took—suddenly I knew exactly what to do. Some-

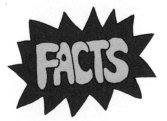

times easy answers are not easy to see. I was lucky that Mimi was there to help me.

The best thing about Mimi's idea was that after I fixed the title, it looked even better than before. Sometimes that can happen with mistakes.

THE NEW THING I WAS SUDDENLY THINKING ABOUT AFTER MIMI LEFT

That simple ideas are sometimes better than complicated ideas.

WHAT MY BRAIN THOUGHT OF

I KNOW HOW TO GET RID OF THE RECYCLING CONTAINER!

SOMETIMES A NEW GOOD IDEA CAN MAKE YOU JUMP UP AND DOWN LIKE AN EXCITED MR. SCRUFFERS.

Even though the good deed thing was working, I knew it still wasn't right. A happy ghost is still a ghost, and to make everything right I needed the ghost to be gone, and gone forever!

THE SPECIAL GUEST

Mimi and I had to carry our project and Marvin to school for our presentation. It was not easy to carry all that stuff without dropping anything. It made me wonder if Marvin was worried.

TWO LUCKY THINGS

I'm not usually excited to see Sammy first thing in the morning, but today things were different. I couldn't wait to get to school and find him. I made Mimi walk faster than usual, but I was lucky—she didn't ask why. When we got to school she saw Grace F. on the playground and wanted to stop and talk with her. That was lucky again, because now I could go and find Sammy by myself.

Sammy was not very hard to find. His favorite jacket is bright orange. When someone is wearing a bright orange jacket, he is easy to see.

THE NOTE

Right after I gave Sammy the note he said, "That's too bad—I was kind of getting to like the ghost, but Mr. Woods will be happy." I thought about what he said, but forced myself to shake my head. I was kind of liking the ghost too, but it was wrong to keep the lie going. We had to get rid of it.

Sammy took the note and promised he would give it to Mr. Woods. I made him put

his hand over his heart when he promised, because after what he'd just said, I didn't want
him changing his mind.

WHAT THE NOTE SAID

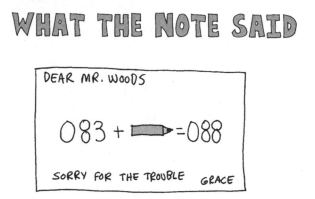

THE SURPRISE IN MISS LOIS'S CLASS

After we all were sitting in our seats, Miss
Lois said, "I have a special treat for you. Our
surprise guest is here." Of course instantly
everyone was paying attention. What she
said next was not what anyone was expecting. "Our guest is the earth," said Miss Lois.

The earth is not a normal guest. Miss Lois went over to the door and opened it, and in walked Mr. Frank dressed up like the earth.

At first everyone was too surprised to speak, but then a few seconds later, we all jumped out of our seats and ran up to him. It was double love for me.

Mr. Frank is everyone's favorite almost-teacher. We all know him because he used to be the student teacher in our classroom and now he is studying to get his teaching certificate. Once he is a real teacher everyone is hoping he will come back and teach us again. It was great to see him. Miss Lois was right—he was an excellent surprise. After everyone had talked to him for a few minutes, Miss Lois made us all sit down again. She loves the earth, so seeing Mr. Frank in the earth costume was probably helping her to be in a good mood. When we were all quiet, she said, "Mr. Frank is going to help us take a mini quiz about the world." Usually no one likes quizzes, but a quiz with your favorite teacher dressed up as the earth is not a normal quiz.

Having the earth in your classroom makes it a lot more exciting. Miss Lois gave out the test papers, and then we started.

WHAT WAS HARD

It was hard to be serious and not laugh while we were taking the test. I kept imagining that it would be funny if Mr. Frank started dancing. A dancing earth is something that I'd like to see.

After the quiz Mr. Frank came around and we had to tell him the facts we had learned for our assignment. If we got them right and did a good job, he gave us a pencil and a sticker. Pretty much everyone did a good job except for Owen 1 and Robert Walters. They got mixed up and did their project on the wrong continent. Instead of finding facts for Asia, they found them for Australia. At first I though Miss Lois was going to be mad, but she surprised me and said it was okay. They were probably the most lucky that Mr. Frank was there to help her be in a good mood.

WHAT I CAN'T WAIT TO SEE

Right before lunch Miss Lois had us all stand with Mr. Frank so she could take a photo, and the best part is that we are each going to get a copy to put in our earth books to keep. Mimi and I got a really good spot right next to him on the South America side. That was extra lucky, because that's what our project was about.

MY SURPRISE AT LUNCH

It wasn't as fancy as Sunni's bento lunches, but I loved it. Sometimes even just a little surprise can seem huge when you are 100 percent not expecting it.

185
• • • • •

WHAT HAPPENED AT LUNCH

After we finished eating, Mimi wanted to go and look for the recycling bin. I followed her through every hall in the school, but we couldn't find it. "It's gone," said Mimi. She sounded disappointed, but I wasn't. I was the exact opposite, and that was because we were standing in front of the principal's office right in front of a recycling bin with the number 088 on it.

I THINK IT'S GONE FOR GOOD.

UH-HUH.

ME TRYING NOT TO SMILE

I thought Mimi would say something else about the recycling bin, but she didn't. Instead she changed the subject and said, "Race you to the front doors." We aren't allowed to run in school, but no one was around, so I nodded. "Three, two, one," said Mimi, and then we took off. I'm usually faster than Mimi, but I let her win. It was one of those things that made her happy and me happy both at the same time.

WHAT IS HARD TO DO

It's hard to be brave, especially if being brave will get you into trouble, but sometimes it's worth taking a chance. When I was walking home with Mimi and Marvin, I made a list of all the things I had been brave about. There were only two things on the list, the beetle and the raccoobat.

WHAT IS BETTER THAN A LIST WITH TWO BRAVE THINGS ON IT

A list with three brave things, so I took a big breath and said . . .

After I said it, I closed my eyes and tried not to look at Mimi. She was quiet and not saying anything, so finally I opened my eyes to see what was going on.

WHAT MIMI'S FACE DID NOT LOOK LIKE

WHAT MIMI'S FACE LOOKED LIKE

I couldn't believe it. She wasn't mad, and she didn't look one bit surprised. "I thought so," said Mimi. "I don't believe in ghosts, plus you're not a very good liar." "I'm not?" I asked. Mimi shook her head. This was good news. I didn't want to be a good liar. In fact, I wanted to be the worst liar in the whole world. If there was a trophy for that, I wanted to win it.

Thinking about the trophy made me imagine some other imaginary trophies. Life isn't fair—if it was there would be trophies for a lot more things than sports and spelling tests.

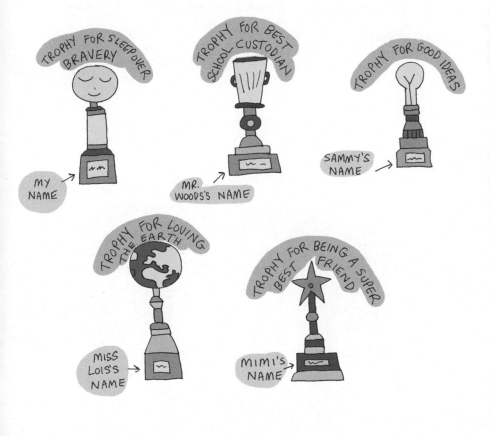

TROPHY FOR SLEEPOVER BRAVERY

MY NAME →

TROPHY FOR BEST SCHOOL CUSTODIAN

MR. WOODS'S NAME →

TROPHY FOR GOOD IDEAS

SAMMY'S NAME →

TROPHY FOR LOVING THE EARTH

MISS LOIS'S NAME →

TROPHY FOR BEING A SUPER BEST FRIEND

MIMI'S NAME →

For the whole rest of the walk home, Mimi and I talked about the lie and the ghost. Some of it made me uncomfortable, but some of it was funny, too. When we got to my house there was only one thing I wanted to do: give a hug to my almost-like-a-sister best friend. That was my best idea.

WHAT GRACE WILL BE THINKING ABOUT IN HER NEXT BOOK